An untold story, the Christmas Fairy

Published in the United States
by Diane Alber Art LLC
ISBN: 978-1-960643-39-1
For more information, or to book an event,
visit our website:
www.dianealber.com
Printed in China

Have you ever heard of the

Christmas Fairy!

No?

Well, I'm not as famous as some other fairies YET...

But wait till you hear what I started doing to make Christmas extra special!

I'm not sure if you know this, but my job is to help Santa inspect and organize the presents each year.

Before I came along,
Santa's system was a

mess!

Some gifts were

DAMAGED

during transit...

Turns out reindeer love to
nibble on wrapping paper!

Some were stacked

TOO HIGH

they would fall over in the middle of the night!

Imagine the racket!

And now, since I've been in charge of stacking and inspecting presents things are looking amazing!

But then I noticed a new problem, children were finding their gifts so easily on Christmas morning...

And they were opening their presents way too **FAST,** they barely had a chance to enjoy the holiday!

Wrapping paper and ribbons were flying everywhere like confetti!

That's when I got an idea! What if I hid one of the presents and made it into a fun game? A scavenger hunt with clues would make the joy of opening presents last even longer!

It could transform Christmas morning into an
unforgettable adventure!

With a flick of my wand and a sparkle in my step, I set off to hide a present!

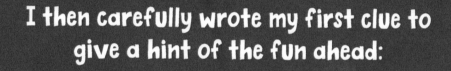

I then carefully wrote my first clue to
give a hint of the fun ahead:

The Christmas Fairy hid a present this year,
it may be far or it may be near.
But don't you worry, there's good news,
she took the time to leave some clues.

As I fluttered around the house, leaving
a trail of clues. I giggled to myself,
imagining the childrens excitement as
they tried to figure out each one.

Santa watched me work
and chuckled, "Great job!"
as he gave me a high five
as I flew by.

I was able to hide presents
at three houses that year!

The next morning I watched my plan in action! At the first house Anthony was in shock to find a clue!

This clue is hiding, it's not in the air. It's closer to the ground, by your favorite chair.

At the second house Sofia was surprised to find a clue waiting for her!

This note's chilly,
but it's not outside.
Look where milk
would hide.

She immediately ran into the refrigerator to find the next clue hidden under the orange juice.

And I can't forget
the third house!
Tommy was probably the most
excited about his clue!

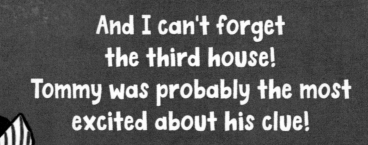

If you're looking for a
clue that's really neat,
check inside something
that covers your feet.

He immediately started searching through his big pile of shoes. There, tucked in his favorite red sneaker, was the next clue, curled up like a tiny scroll.

The children **LOVED IT!**
The next year I picked a few more houses to hide presents
and leave clues.

News traveled like a snowflake in the wind, and
before I knew it, I was actually getting letters
from kids asking me to hide their presents!

They would leave their letter for me right next to
Santa's letter! Can you believe it!?!

It didn't take long for hundreds of children to write letters requesting me to hide presents!

It was unbelievable!

I knew I needed to get help! So I asked my
fairy friends to join in on the fun!

They were so excited!

Now every Christmas hundreds of children all over the world wake up to find clues!

Under doormats!

In cereal boxes!

So, this Christmas, if you want to add a sprinkle of joy to your holiday, just write me a note requesting me to come! And I will try my best to visit!

Parents,

If you're not quite sure how to invite the Christmas Fairy to your home, please check out the free printable with helpful information on how to invite her and get your house ready for her visit! www.dianealber.com

Made in the USA
Las Vegas, NV
16 December 2024

14482578R10021